Zephyr TAKES Flight

STEVE LIGHT

WALKER BOOKS
AND SUBSIDIARIES

LONDON · BOSTON · SYDNEY · AUCKLAND

Zephyr loved aeroplanes.

She drew pictures of them,

made them out of paper

and built them out of junk.

Mostly, she played with them.

One day, she hoped to fly one of her own.

"Grandma! Look at my plane!" Zephyr shouted.

But Grandma was reading the paper.

"Daddy, play aeroplanes with me!"
said Zephyr.

"Not now," said Daddy.

"I'm busy."

Zephyr went to find Mum, but she was busy, too.

So Zephyr tried her **triple loop-de-loop spectacular**

Zephyr was in trouble.

In her room, she folded a paper aeroplane and sent it zipping through the air. It landed behind the chest of drawers.

There was something
back there!

It was a door...

This was surely the most wondrous place Zephyr had ever seen.

It was filled with papers and pens, drawings and maps,
books about how to fly and where to go.

And then there were the flying machines.
There were big ones and small ones, some with propellers and some
with rudders and very strange things. And all of them were real.

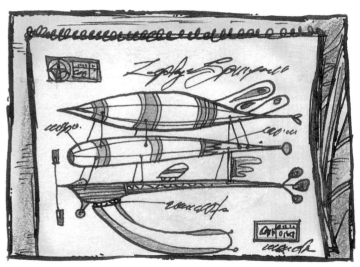

Zephyr had an idea…

She climbed aboard the FS *Bessie*. She flicked the switches.

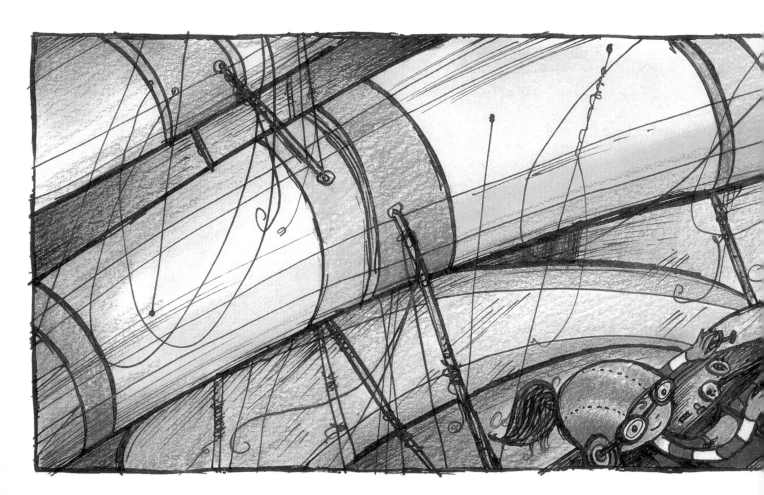

The engine creaked and cranked and finally started.

Her **triple loop-de-loop spectacular** was much more fun in the sky!

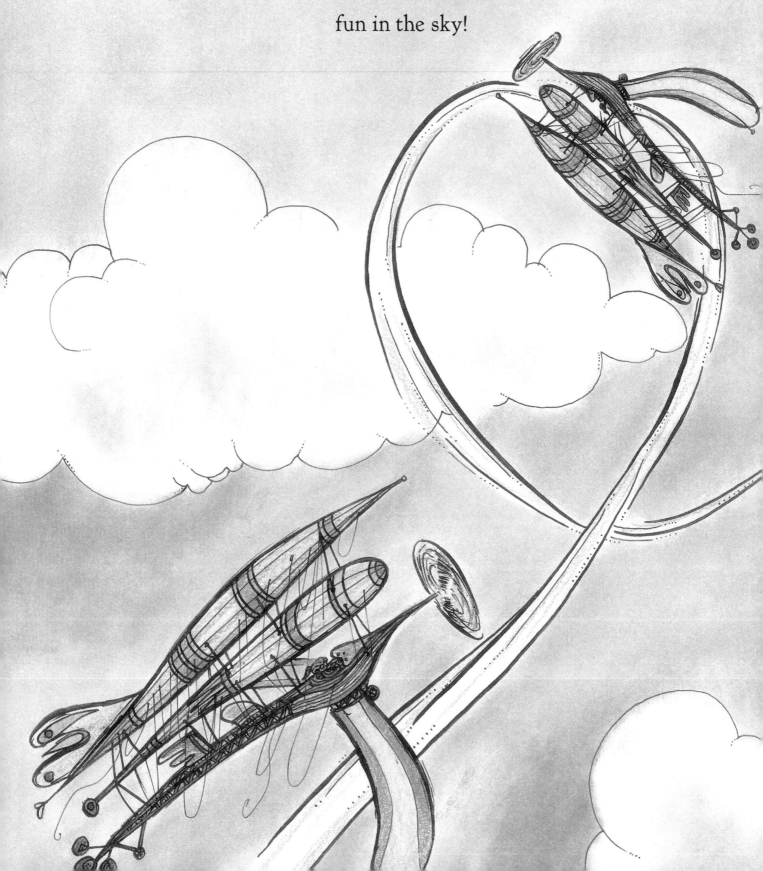

Putt-putt, sputter-sputter.

Oh, no!

The engine coughed and went quiet.

The FS *Bessie* drifted lower and lower.

Zephyr held on tight.

BUMP!

The plane landed. *What is this place?* thought Zephyr.

She had never seen mountains so high, skies so blue, trees so lush.

And in the distance ...

flying pigs!

As Zephyr hurried towards the village,
one small pig ran along beside her.

The little pig said his name was Rumbus.

He could not fly.

Zephyr felt sad for the little pig.

Flying was a wonderful thing!

Then she had an idea…

Zephyr measured
and folded.

Zephyr drew
and cut.

Then Rumbus
took a running start ...

and he flew!

"Do a **triple loop-de-loop spectacular!**" called Zephyr.

Zephyr was happy to see Rumbus fly with his family
for the first time.

Zephyr thought of her own family.

It was time to go home.

She'd need help from her new friend.

Rumbus had an idea.

"Zephyr!
Come and have your pancakes!"
called Daddy.

Zephyr ran to breakfast and had a ...

triple-hug, triple-pancake spectacular!

To Mia and Emily – my inspirations for Zephyr

First published 2012 by Walker Books Ltd
87 Vauxhall Walk, London SE11 5HJ

2 4 6 8 10 9 7 5 3 1

© 2012 Steve Light

The right of Steve Light to be identified as author/illustrator of this work has been asserted by
him in accordance with the Copyright, Designs and Patents Act 1988

This book has been typeset in Kennerly

Printed in China

British Library Cataloguing in Publication Data:
a catalogue record for this book is available from the British Library

ISBN 978-1-4063-4029-7

www.walker.co.uk